Printed in the U.S.A.

ISBN 0-7172-8268-6

JIM HENSON'S MUPPETS
IN

Fozzie Bear,
Star Helper

A Book About Responsibility

By Bonnie Worth • Illustrated by David Prebenna

GROLIER

It was a typical day at the Bear house. Mr. Bear was repairing a lamp that baby Freddie had broken. Mrs. Bear was at her computer making a chart for work. Baby Freddie was exploring.

Fozzie Bear was on the living-room floor
sticking silly stickers into his silly-sticker
album when the front doorbell chimed.
Dingdong!

"I'll get it!" called Fozzie.

But his mom beat him to it and—oops!—tripped over Fozzie's baseball bat and glove, which were lying in the middle of the floor.

"How many times have I told you, Fozzie Bear? Baseball glove on the shelf. Bat in the closet," his mom said.

Fozzie picked up his bat and glove. "Sorry, Mom," he said.

But he couldn't help thinking to himself that ever since his mom had gone back to work after having the baby, she seemed a little grumpy.

It was Kermit at the door. "Want to help paint the clubhouse?" he asked.

"You bet," said Fozzie. He dashed upstairs to change into an old shirt and pair of pants.

"Don't forget to pick up your album and stickers off the floor!" his mom called after him.

But Fozzie was so eager to get to the clubhouse that he forgot to pick up his sticker stuff.

And while Fozzie was at the clubhouse, baby Freddie was home...getting into mischief. Freddie had gotten into his big brother's stickers and made a sticky, icky mess.

When Fozzie got home, his dad was waiting for him. "Didn't Mom tell you to pick up your sticker album before you left the house?" he asked sternly.

"Uh-oh," said Fozzie. "I guess I forgot."

So Fozzie spent that evening helping his dad unpeel the stickers.

It wasn't much fun.

Later that night, just as Fozzie was climb-
ing into bed, he heard his mom cry out.
"Who left the cap off the toothpaste?"

Baby Freddie had gotten into the tooth-paste . . . and made a sticky, icky, *yicky* mess!

"Uh-oh," said Fozzie Bear, standing in the bathroom doorway and staring around. The walls, floor, tub, sink . . . everything was covered with toothpaste.

"I guess I forgot," sighed Fozzie. "Again."

Fozzie sleepily helped his folks clean up the mess. Washing dried toothpaste off the bathtub was no fun at all.

Afterward, they all went downstairs to have a cup of hot chocolate . . . and a little talk.

"You're a big kid now," his dad said, between sips of chocolate. "It's time you learned to take some responsibility. Especially now that Freddie's getting into everything."

"What's responsibility mean?" Fozzie asked.

"Responsibility," his mom explained, "means remembering to do the things you're supposed to do without having to be told all the time."

As his dad was tucking him into bed, Fozzie asked him, "What happens if I try really hard to be responsible, and I still forget?"

"I guess you'll just have to work even harder at it," his dad replied.

"But work's no fun," Fozzie pouted.

"That's not always true," his dad said. "I have lots of fun at work."

Fozzie kissed his dad good-night.

"See?" his dad said. "You didn't forget to kiss me good-night."

"That's because I like to kiss you good-night," Fozzie grinned sleepily. "I don't like to pick up my stuff."

At recess the next day, Fozzie told his friends about his troubles at home.

"Once when I kept forgetting to bring my library book back, my mother made me a chart," Kermit told him.

"What's a chart?" Fozzie asked.

"A chart measures things," Kermit said. "Like how much money a business makes in a year. Or how much rain falls in a month. Or—"

"—how often I do my chores in a week!" Fozzie broke in excitedly.

Fozzie was so happy about the idea of a chart that he raced home after school.

"Mom?" he called as he opened the front door. "Could you help me make a chart? A chart that helps me remember to do my chores?"

Mrs. Bear was only too delighted. Together they sat down at her computer. And this is what they came up with:

FOZZIE'S CHORES	DAY OF THE WEEK						
	S	M	T	W	Th	F	Sa
PICK UP CLOTHES							
PUT TOYS AWAY							
PICK UP BAT AND GLOVE							
MAKE BED							
SET TABLE							

The next day, Mrs. Bear bought a box of sticker stars.

First Fozzie made his bed. He got a gold star on his chart.

Then he built a castle of blocks and afterward put the blocks away himself. He got a blue star for that.

Later on, Fozzie put some new silly stickers in his album and remembered to put the album on the shelf, away from Freddie...for a red star.

Over the next few days, Fozzie put the cap on the toothpaste, his baseball bat in the closet, his baseball glove on the shelf, and all his dirty clothes in the laundry. He even wrote in new chores just so he could get more stars...like helping Freddie put on his clothes...helping Freddie eat his cereal...and showing Freddie how to put away *his* blocks.

"Because," Fozzie said to his little brother, "you're never too young to learn about responsibility!"

At the end of the week, Fozzie counted his stars. There were twenty-five of them!

For dessert that night, his mom baked him a banana cream cake—his favorite. She decorated it with stars.

"Because you're a real star," his dad said, giving him a hug. "A star helper!"

Let's Talk About Responsibility

Responsibility is a big word. And being responsible can sometimes feel like a big chore. But think about it from a grown-up's point of view. If you were Fozzie's mom and you had just tripped over his things, wouldn't you be a little upset?

Besides, as Fozzie finds out, it can feel nice to be responsible.

Here are some questions about responsibility for you to think about:

What does the word responsibility mean to you?

How can you be more responsible around your house?

Can you think of some ways to help you remember your responsibilities?